PAIR-IT BOOKS™

It's Raining!

Written by Sarah Vazquez

STECK-VAUGHN
ELEMENTARY · SECONDARY · ADULT · LIBRARY

A Harcourt Classroom Education Company

www.steck-vaughn.com

It's raining.

I will get my umbrella.

I will get my jacket.

I will get my hat.

I will get my rain suit.

I will get my boots.

We will get wet!